M. G. T.

The Finished Web.

A novel

M. G. T.

The Finished Web.
A novel

ISBN/EAN: 9783337001223

Printed in Europe, USA, Canada, Australia, Japan

Cover: Foto ©Andreas Hilbeck / pixelio.de

More available books at **www.hansebooks.com**

THE FINISHED WEB.

BY M. G. T.

CHAPTER I.

Miss Margaret Stanhill, only daughter of one of San Francisco's millionaires, was feeling just a little low-spirited. Yesterday she arrived from the East with her father, and the home-coming had saddened her. There had been no one to welcome her but the servants. This fine old house, as complete in all details as taste and money could make it, had depressed her. She was not sure that she liked elegance. The gardens around the house provoked her; the borders and beds were so painfully regular. She preferred old-fashioned gardens with a little of everything growing in them; and with rose bushes that were not so fashionably trimmed.

Then the neighboring houses tired her; they were all so very big. Everything seemed new and strange. She had left it all when she was 5 years old, and she was 20 now. Her life there did not seem to belong to her. Only two things could she remember of it—her mother and her mother's love for herself. The last time she had seen her mother had been just before she left home. How clearly she remembered it! She thrilled even now as she recalled the fondness of the embrace, the tenderness of the kiss, that last embrace, that last kiss!

" Don't forget to love me," her mother had whispered, " and don't forget to be good to your brother, my little Pearl."

Her mother's eyes had been large and dark and very sad. They often haunted her. She had always wished some one would talk to her about her mother. Several times she had spoken of her to her father, but he had never answered her. She had not resented this. With a woman's tenderness she had said to herself, "How well he loved her! He can not bear to speak of her after all these years!"

From Frisco she had been taken East and placed in a Convent. There she was completely separated from the brother whom her mother had bidden her be good to. He was then three years younger than herself. She had never heard from him during all these years. She had not even seen a picture of him, nor had she seen her father often while she was at school.

After having graduated she went to Europe to be "finished off." This period of her life had been particularly delightful; it was her first sight of the world.

Six months ago she had returned to New York City. Her father met her there and treated her with the utmost care and consideration. She had been given a splendid suite of rooms, a bank account, and was introduced into society.

Margaret Stanhill would have been called very pretty under any circumstances, as it was she became the reigning beauty of the season.

She was a charming girl. A blonde, well formed, with sweet modest ways. She had various accomplishments, not the smallest of which was a knack of making friends with her own sex.

Women seemed to love her naturally. They were never jealous of her, for in no case did she try to supplant them.

Of men she did not think very well.

Her most intimate friend, the chaperone with whom she had been abroad, advocated woman's rights. Perhaps Margaret had inherited some of her ideas.

She had very decided ideas of her own, however, and did not feel greatly impressed with the " beaux " who were prepared to worship at her shrine.

At the end of the season she had grown weary of society and rejoiced when her father set the day for their return home.

She had expected to see her brother when she arrived. She had pictured their meeting so often of late.

With her father she had never felt altogether at her ease. He treated her kindly, but he was so cool and crisp in his manner. Why did he not talk to her of her brother? Could it be that the boy had angered him in some way? ..

That noon Margaret and her father lunched together.

"Are you comfortable, my dear?" he asked, and his tone was unusually affectionate. "Can I do anything to add to your happiness in any way?" Quick to catch the tender note, Margaret answered impulsively:

"When shall I see Valance, father?"

"Your brother is at school," her father said, coldly and shortly. "Perhaps if you are here in the summer, you can see him."

CHAPTER II.

In quite a different part of 'Frisco, in a shabby little furnished room, was another woman. She was writing in an old-fashioned diary.

"Fifteen years! I am growing weary of living in hope! What hope have I anyway? To-day I read in the Society notes that the beautiful Miss Stanhill had returned to 'Frisco. My little Margaret, my little Pearl! How long ago it seems since I last kissed her! I can hear her father's voice even now, saying sternly: 'Go! You shall never see your children again! For the sake of my own name, which you bear, I will not expose you, but if you ever dare approach to make yourself known to your children I will brand you as an infamous woman. They shall be taught that you are dead.'"

Here the writing ceased and the writer bowed her head upon her hands.

· As I am not trying to unravel a mystery, only recording certain events in the lives of the people I am writing of, I shall explain why Mrs. Stanhill, the wife of a millionaire, is thus supposed to be dead while she sits grieving in her shabby room on Mission street.

When Mlle. Marie Le Martin was asked in marriage by Valance Stanhill of San Francisco she was only sixteen.

Her parents lived in Los Gatos. They accepted the offer immediately, and in a wonderfully short space of time the little unformed girl became the millionaire's wife.

Valance Stanhill was just thirty-six. He had made his money and his position for himself. He was passionately in love with his young wife.

Marie was scarcely fitted to be mistress of her husband's fine home. She did not care for society, her life till she became a mother was a most miserable one.

At first she had tried to understand this man who had pretended to love her so, but she finally gave it up. She was always obedient and quiet.

Valance Stanhill thought it right to absorb his wife. She ceased to be a daughter, she was not allowed to visit her parents and they were not allowed to visit her. In two years they both died.

Valance Stanhill's one intimate friend was a Frenchman. He spent a great deal of his time with them, he was a man of lax morals, and thought it was no dishonor to conceive a passion for another man's wife.

He quickly saw how matters stood; that Marie did not feel that perfect love for her husband that "casteth out all fear;" that love which is at all times a wife's surest safeguard.

He won her confidence by degrees.

Poor Marie believed him to be a God-sent brother to her. She took comfort in his society.

Her husband became more and more unbearable. He took it for granted that she would be his slave.

Still Alfred Critien did not dare speak of his love to her!

Valance, her second child, was born. She became more of a child-worshipper than ever, all her hopes were centred in her little ones. If she had been permitted to nurse them day and night she would have been satisfied, but her husband was jealous even of the children.

As his wife she must take part in society. She must parade her beauty and wear her diamonds.

When they went out he was sure to find something to lecture her about. Then Alfred Critien would find out all about it and comfort her the next day.

One evening when little Val was three months old, Mr. Stanhill came home earlier than usual. Entering with his latch key, he went to look for his wife, as he neared the sitting room he heard voices. Stopping cautiously, he listened. then applied his eye to the key hole. He beheld his wife weeping and Alfred Critien was kneeling beside her. He waited for no more, he would not make a fool of himself, he would not mention what he had seen to his friend. He always believed woman to be to blame in such cases.

He went to his room.

When Critien left the house, he sent for his wife and declared that he *knew* of her dishonor. He further avowed his belief that Val was not his child. He absolutely refused to allow her to vindicate herself in any way. Then he said the cruel words chronicled in her diary. She had accepted them as the death-knell of her earthly hope of happiness.

In after years Marie wondered that she had acted as she did.

She had been so shocked, so dazed!

In her own sight, in the sight of God, she knew herself to be innocent, even in thought, but she felt incapable of acting for herself. This shame her husband believed her to be capable of was such a terrible thing! The very thought of it made her brain grow dizzy.

Then her pride came to her aid. Yes, she would go! God would avenge her some day.

Oh, the many miserable souls that are waiting for that day!

She felt herself to be a martyr. She took off her jewels, and dressed herself in her plainest dress. She went to the nursery to kiss her children. Baby Val was asleep, with his little fat thumb in his mouth. She paused to admire him.

O! if she might take him with her! She gathered him in her arms and started for the door. Her husband blocked the way.

"Give him to me," she prayed, "you have insulted him, too!"

But Valance Stanhill only smiled scornfully.

"No, that shall be your punishment. I shall always hate the boy, but you shall not have him, and neither shall his father!"

Little Margaret ran up to her. Holding her to her heart she had whispered the words the child never forgot.

Then she left the house.

She had now here to go. No money in her pocket. She walked on and on.

She reached Market street. It was crowded. Shop girls were hurrying home. It made her more desolate to look at them! She was homeless!

Finally she could walk no further. Her strength was leaving her. The world about her seemed to stagger; she fainted.

Three weeks later she came to herself. She was in a hospital. In another week she would be turned out into the world again. What was she to do? She heard women talking near her. They were speaking of how hard it was to get help in the country.

"Why," said one, "they will take almost any one and never so much as hint after her references!"

Marie asked for a newspaper and looked

through the advertisements. One read: "A companion for an invalid wanted; good country home."

She obtained a postal card and sent in an application for the place.

In a few days she received the answer. She was to apply on the tenth. That would be the day after she should leave the hospital. She asked to stay a day longer, and was allowed to do so.

On the day of her departure she felt very weak and miserable. When she went to the glass to put on her hat she hardly knew herself. Her hair was gray, her face pale and thin. She was no longer a beautiful woman!

On her way to the appointment she passed a lawyer's office. The sign read, "Consultation free." She went in and stated her case, only suppressing names.

The lawyer told her she could not get her children. Had she tried at first she might have had the youngest. She had left her husband's house. While he could support the children he could keep them. Did she want a divorce, and what were her grounds?

Her interview with the advertiser was satisfactory, and that evening she went to a neighboring country town.

Her employer was an old lady.

She stayed with her for five years, then the poor old soul died.

Marie returned to 'Frisco and entered the hospital for trained nurses.

She assumed the little white cap and apron and soon found comfort in her work.

Lately she had left the hospital and joined the Alpha Association.

And there we find her in a dingy, cheerless room. a patient, gray-haired woman, suffering unmerited crucifixion, as are many others of her sex to-day.

Her desolation had not hardened her heart, she did not cry out "There is no God," but something of the "peace this world can not give" had stolen into her pure soul, and she lived for the good she might do.

CHAPTER III.

The Stanhill residence was ablaze with light. Miss Stanhill was about to celebrate her twenty-first birthday.

The stately hall and drawing-rooms were hung with costly flowers.

The guests, the elite of 'Frisco's society, were arriving.

Miss Stanhill stood beside her father receiving them, and most beautiful did she look in her gown of soft, creamy lace.

Her father was growing prouder and prouder of her each day.

It was a year since she had returned to 'Frisco. She was very much "at home" now and had a great many friends and admirers.

Miss Stanhill was a revelation to California society. Not so much because of her exceeding fairness, California belles are always handsome, but here was a millionaire's daughter who took pleasure in seeing other women shine socially; who listened to no scandal; who defended every woman's good name. She was not easily flattered; took every one good-naturedly.

Just how she kept herself so pure and unspotted, I do not know. Only to look into her sweet, serious eyes was a lesson in itself.

Margaret was a natural hostess. She was never so much in her element as when helping people have a good time.

The ball was a success. Supper was over; the german also. Chaperones were beginning to look tired behind their fans. Second and third year rosebuds were hunting for their wraps. A sprinkling of debutantes were still dancing away as if they could never grow weary.

Margaret was passing through the hall when she saw a servant with a dispatch in her hand. Taking it, she looked at the postmark and turned pale. It was from S. College. Something was the matter with her brother!

She hastened to find her father. He was in the smoking room. He opened the telegram leisurely, read it, then handed it to her, seeing by her face that she expected it. It read:

" Your son is very much worse."

Mr. Stanhill left the room and Margaret followed him.

" You knew that Valance was ill, and did not tell me," she said, looking steadily into his eyes. He did not answer her.

" You will go by the first train?" she continued.

"No! Why should I? He has typhoid fever, and there is danger of contagion. He is well looked after. No expense will be spared," answered the father hurriedly.

But Margaret was thoroughly aroused. She said, sternly:

"Why should you? Because he is your son. O! how can you think of contagion! If my mother was alive would she think of it? You say you will not go. Very well, I shall go myself," and then she turned and left the room.

Valance Stanhill was completely surprised. This from a little girl who had never argued a point with him before.

Somehow he admired her for it, though. " Go to the college herself;" indeed, she should not! In the morning he would speak to her about it.

But when the morning came, at 10 o'clock, when he sent to ask for an interview, he found that she had gone by the 7 o'clock train.

And to his dispatch of " Return immediately," she answered:

" My brother needs me and I shall not leave him."

And then was he forced into submission.   .

CHAPTER IV.

" You will have to get a nurse. You will not be able to stand it day and night. It will be weeks before he is better," said the college doctor.

Margaret Stanhill had been three days with her sick brother. It was pitiful to see him toss about unconscious of everything about him.

How wicked she felt when she remembered how she had neglected her mother's last request so long. Of course it had not been her fault entirely, but she should have asserted herself long ago.

Poor Valance! How big and black his eyes were! So like their dead mother's. Suppose he should die! Would that mother forgive her?

She did not want a nurse. She would take care of him herself. But of course she would break down if she didn't have one. She had promised God to devote herself to Valance if only his dear life was spared her, and she would do it. Her father should be forced to do his duty, or answer to her for it.

So a message was wired by the doctor to the Alpha Association of trained nurses in 'Frisco, and God allowed it to be Marie Stanhill, or Mrs. Hill, as she was called, who was the nurse selected to be sent.

And O! how the mother thanked God for this privilege. To be near her boy in his last moments; or if He saw best, nurse him back to life.

But could she stand it thus to be near her darlings and not cry out her claim upon them? Yes, for their sakes she felt that she could. It would be best for them not to know. They believed her to be dead, and it would do no good to undeceive them. She was old, and they did not know her. She could bear it.

When she first beheld her little Pearl, so glorious in her pure young womanhood, the goodness of her soul looking from her eyes, that gave her courage. She could have knelt at her feet, but she could not tell her that her mother had been suspected of evil-doing by her father and driven from his home. Innocent as she knew herself to be, she could not tell her. Besides she had no proof of her innocence. And then her daughter might not believe in her.

The hardest part of her trial came when she stood beside the bed of her baby, her darling Val. To see him toss with pain, and not be able to gather him into her arms! Not be able to kiss his parched lips! O, it was so bitterly hard!

But her face was calm, and she listened silently to her daughter's orders. She was cautioned to take care of her own child; "O Nurse!" cried Margaret, "only help me bring him back to health, and there is nothing I will not do for you!"

Thus together did mother and sister care for poor, lonely Val, while the days and weeks passed by. Such days and weeks they were to the poor, mother! So full of anxiety for the sick boy, and so precious because spent near her darling. She thanked God again and again that she was permitted to know what a grand woman her little Pearl had become!

Margaret grew very fond of the quiet nurse.

How pleasant it would be to have her for a companion; she spoke to her about it.

"I have no real friend," she said; "money does not buy affection. I feel that I could trust you so."

One day the doctor said that at 4 o'clock the next morning the patient would gain consciousness, and be either very much better or sink rapidly; it was the turning point of the disease.

"Of course I shall take the second watch," said Margaret, as the doctor left.

At midnight she came into the sick room and kindly but decidedly dismissed the nurse. With not a word she was obeyed.

Once in her own room, the mother threw herself upon her knees to pray for her boy. Sleep! Ah! when can a true mother sleep when her child is in danger.

The hours finally passed. It was half after three; she felt that she must go to her child. What if he should be dying! She wrung her hands in anguish.

Noiselessly she entered the sick room. Beside the bed Margaret was fast asleep—nature had proved too strong for her.

The mother went to the sick boy, and her practised eye noted the change. He was better. He stirred feebly, and opened his eyes, a wan smile came to his lips, and he whispered, "Mother!"

With a great effort Marie controlled herself

and gave him some water. As her hand touched his he turned and kissed it.

"You were dreaming," she faltered. Only
God knew how hard it was to say it.

"Of my dead mother," he answered in a
weak voice. Then he smiled and fell asleep
like a tired child.

Margaret awoke with a start. "He came back
to me and I was asleep! Is he better? O, will
he live?" she cried brokenly.

"He is better, dear," the nurse said gently;
"he will live, thank God."

Then something made Margaret put her arms
around the nurse, and together they mingled
their tears of thankfulness.

One week later the nurse left quietly without
receiving her wages.

Very much distressed Margaret sent her a
check for $500, in care of the Alpha Associa-
tion; she also asked for her address. The
matron wrote that Mrs. Hill on receipt of money
had left the city.

CHAPTER V.

Mr. Valance Stanhill sat reading a telegram
he had just received from his daughter. It ran
thus:

"Have things ready for us. We will arrive
to-night. Meet us at the depot."

During the last few weeks he had been bat-
tling with himself. How should he act? He could

not refuse to be civil to this boy whom he had
acknowledged as his son without giving a reason for it. He simply would not tell Margaret
her mother's miserable story. Her mother whom
she believed to be dead. She might demand
proof of what he said; he had not waited for
proof. Margaret, his own darling, might hate
him! How she had spoken to him that night!

He had admired her for it. "A chip of the
old block," he said to himself. Yes, he must
give in to her, he must be civil to the boy.

He would soon be well enough to return to
school. He would send him abroad as soon as
possible.

So he ordered the carriage and was at the
depot in time for the arrival.

* * * * * * *

All the devotion of Margaret's heart seemed
to centre itself upon her brother. She made her
sitting room into a bed room for him, and waited upon him night and day. She thought nothing too good for his use.

And how poor, lonely Val loved her! He had
always hungered for affection; it was such joy
to feel himself the object of some one's consideration. He grew to depend more and more upon
her.

She gloried in the fact.

Margaret's character had developed wonderfully of late. She succeeded with her father in
a most remarkable manner. She simply took it

for granted that Val was his first consideration,
that he desired nothing so much as his happiness.

Mr. Stanhill found himself acting the part of
a devoted father. His motives were of a mixed
nature, to begin with he must stand well with
Margaret, and again he believed all women to be
fickle. She would tire of such sisterly devotion
after a while.

But as time went on she did not tire. She
treated Val as her own child. He had been neglected so many years, she must make it up
to him all she could now.

The young man felt his father's coldness.

"He does not care for me," he would say sadly, "but I can bear it while I am with you."

Then brave Margaret would show her affection more than ever.

Society was greatly concerned at Miss Stanhill's seclusion, several heiress-seeking young
men particularly.

Mr Stanhill remonstrated with her himself, but
was convinced when she put her arms around his
neck and said:

"You want me to be happy, don't you, dear?
You don't want to marry me off like most fathers
would?"

Among Margaret's few intimate friends was
little Ida Madden. Just why they were intimate
was a puzzle to many. Perhaps the girl's timid
blue eyes told of an unloved life, the life of an
orphan spent with relatives who were not over
kind to her.

Margaret's big heart reached out after her, and she never lost an opportunity of displaying her feelings.

So it came to pass that Ida spent a great deal of her time at the Stanhill residence.

At first Val was much embarrassed when she came near him. Although past eighteen he knew very little of young ladies. Little sixteen-year-old Ida was very gentle, so he soon forgot to be afraid.

Her millionaire uncle's home was not altogether a satisfactory one. The ladies of the family were society women, they devoted their time to amusement, were very handsome, and rather despised the little unformed girl who had been forced into their home. It was a source of immense surprise to them that the elegant Miss Stanhill should think so much of her. They were prepared to be intimate with Margaret themselves, but she displayed her preference in a most decided manner, and sent invitations to Ida only.

CHAPTER VI.

Val's health did not improve; in spite of all Margaret's care he was no better. He had been at home for four months. In May the doctor ordered valley air.

A house at San Rafael was immediately secured and the motherly Margaret began to make all ready for their departure. A few days before

they left she noticed how sad little Ida was looking. Why should she not take her with them,
the poor little dear?

"Val, dear," she said, "would you mind if I
asked Ida to spend the summer with us? She
looks so lonely."

Val answered in rather a shame-faced way.
Why should he? In truth he was rather glad than
otherwise, only he did not care to say so just then.

So the invitation was given and Ida was made
completely happy.

Mr. Stanhill was altogether displeased with the
proposed removal. He wanted Margaret to go
to Long Branch with him. She put an end to his
hope when she said:

"Val is not well enough for such a trip. Next
year we will go."

She evidently did not intend to be separated
from her darling.

The trip from 'Frisco to San Rafael is at all
times a very charming one. In May it is something never to be forgotten.

Over the bay, surely the loveliest bay in the
world, in the ferry-boat to Sancelito, a little town
that nestles in the foothills, thence by rail. Such
a wealth of green hills, studded with brilliant wild
flowers; such broad pastures covered with graz-
ing cattle. Then grand old Tamalpais mountain
is before you.

San Rafael should be called "City of Roses."
Nowhere in California are these "queens of the
garden" more abundant. They are not satisfied

with being stately bushes; they become gigantic monuments. "Lady Banks" creep to the roof of the tallest houses. Pink, white and golden beauties climb to the tops of the highest trees, and even then throw out their aspiring branches as if they longed to go higher. The air is laden with their perfume.

The place the Stanhills had taken was a real paradise. A Queen Anne cottage, surrounded by sloping lawns and an ideal flower garden. There were tiny summer houses here and there, covered with roses. From its front gallery could be seen old Tamalpais.

"A bit of heaven," said Margaret, as they entered the house. "You surely will get well here, Val darling."

And Val sighed contentedly, and Ida flitted about like some happy butterfly.

Val found in her another slave. She amused him quite as much as Margaret did, and then he felt so manly when he was with her. She had little confiding ways that appealed to him; in short, Val fell in love for the first time and Ida was affected in the same manner.

Such delightful times they had, all three of them. They drove for miles and miles and rambled over the hills, and as Val grew stronger they rode horseback, and thus the summer passed.

Mr. Stanhill had gone to Long Branch alone and his children did not miss him.

The first of September came and Margaret was beginning to get ready for a return home.

Little Ida felt low-spirited and her laugh grew less frequent.

Val began to wonder how it would feel not to have her near him all the time.

One evening Margaret had left the children (as she called them) alone. She had letters to write.

Feeling herself much missed, she hurried through with her letters and in an hour went to join them. They had retreated to one of the rose houses, and she playfully decided to surprise them. As she peeped into the little house a surprise awaited her, for there sat her "children" with their arms about each other in a true-love fashion. Their attitude was not to be mistaken, they seemed blissfully contented.

Margaret slipped gently away. "The two babies! Bless them! They shall tell me of their new-found happiness themselves."

Margaret had never dreamed that they would fall in love with each other, she thought so little of such things herself. What could have put such a notion into their silly heads! Then the more she thought of it the more natural it seemed. They were both her darlings, they *should* get married, after a while, of course. And then this God-meant mother went to building air castles in which her babies were to live.

At dark they came to look for her, to tell her all their hopes. They found her with wide-open arms waiting for them.

"Of course it will be ages before I can have a wife," Val said in a manly voice. "I suppose I

shall go back to school, or maybe, you can per-
suade father to give me a position. You will
look after Ida for me, won't you, Madge?"

CHAPTER VII.

In a week they returned home.

Margaret decided to keep the youthful engagement quiet for a while. It was such a holy thing
in her sight. They both looked up to her and
agreed to everything she said.

Val began to weaken again, and his sister grew
anxious. The best physicians in California were
summoned to consult regarding his case.

When they told her the truth, Margaret felt as if
her heart would break, her dear boy was dying of
consumption! Then she grew calm. His remain-
ing life on earth must be made perfectly happy.

She told her father of the doctor's verdict, also
of Val's engagement to little Ida. He did not
object when he saw she meant the marriage to
take place.

All knowledge of the boy's condition was kept
from him and from his little sweetheart.

Margaret arranged everything.

The millionaire uncle gave a glad consent. A
handsome trousseau was provided and a very
quiet ceremony took place.

How happy the young pair were! They talked
joyfully of the future. "I will soon be well now,"
Val would say.

No trouble ever came near them. Margaret

watched over them as a mother over her little
children, she seemed a part of their love dream.

After a while they had a secret to confide.
"Val's baby!" What a wonderful creature it
would be!

Margaret's heart was filled with rapture; it
would give her something else to live for. It was
her hands that fashioned the tiny garments which
the little stranger was to wear. How tenderly
she sewed on the soft lace that was to touch
the dainty throat.

And when the tiny thing was born, only to
close its little eyes in death, it was Margaret who
grieved most for it. The child-mother's tears
were soon dried, the future looked bright to
her. Margaret alone knew of the coming
shadow.

At last it came, and Val knew that he must go
into another world.

"I can hardly believe it, though, I really feel
better, I am not afraid. O! Madge," he said,
"you have been so good to me! I shall tell
mother all about it. You will take care of my
little wife."

CHAPTER VIII.

Margaret was turning from the family tomb
where her young brother's body had just been put
away to rest. Her heart was full of desolation, in
her eyes there was such supreme grief that no one
of all that vast company of people about her dared
approach her. Her father had left home a month

ago. Margaret felt that he had gone on purpose to miss being present at Val's death-bed. One by one the friends of the family withdrew. Margaret turned to enter her carriage; the old family coachman stood with a sorrowful face holding the door open for her. There was nothing more she could do for her darling here.

The child widow was waiting for her at home; she must go and comfort her.

As she turned, a hand was placed upon her arm; it was the woman who had nursed Val at the college, Mrs. Hill. She was evidently bearing a great cross of sorrow, also; she was draped in mourning as heavy as her own. She felt that she must comfort her; she said nothing, but bent and kissed her cheek and drew her into the carriage. Marie could not resist; she would go with her daughter, cost what it would.

As the carriage went through the city, these two women sat silently holding each other's hands. When the house was reached Margaret spoke for the first time.

" It will comfort me if you will come in for a few moments. Val's wife, poor little child! "

Without a word Marie Stanhill followed her child up the marble steps into the home from which she had been so cruelly driven in years gone by. It was no trial to her, her son's death had numbed her heart, she no longer suffered anything.

Margaret took her into her own room. Ida was asleep, they would see her later.

"O, Mrs. Hill, I can not explain it, but it comforts me to be near you! Can you understand it?"

Then she told her all her sorrows. Of Val's life and love; of the little baby who came and went, and of her grief when it died.

"I felt as my mother would have felt," Margaret said; "perhaps her spirit grew through me."

Marie Stanhill listened, and her heart grew heavier each moment. Finally she could stand it no longer and nature came to her relief: she fainted.

Margaret was stricken with remorse; dear, tender Margaret. How she accused herself! How selfish she thought herself! This poor soul had a sorrow of her own, and she had not stopped to inquire into it.

She put her upon her own bed and gave her restoratives.

When the mother opened her eyes her child was bending over her.

"O, do forgive me, Mrs. Hill, for being so selfish in my grief, and tell me of your troubles that I may comfort you."

From that day a light came into Marie Stanhill's darkened life. A friendship was cemented between the two whom God had joined together by the closest and holiest tie on earth or in heaven.

Marie went back to her life as a nurse; she did not come again to her daughter's house, but Margaret visited her each Sunday, and oh, what joy those visits were to the lonely mother.

Together they visited Val's resting place,

" Somehow I feel better when you are here with me," Margaret said one evening as they left the cemetery. "Why am I so sure of sympathy?"

Of her own grief Mrs. Hill would not speak, and with ready tact Margaret discovered that such was the case.

Val's widow became drawn to his sister each day. Mr. Stanhill proposed settling a handsome income upon her, and allowing her to return to her uncle's home, but Margaret refused indignantly.

"She shall stay with me till she asks to leave," she said. "As to an income, my own is enough for both of us."

After her first grief had passed away, the girl-widow became happy. Margaret induced her to study and practise, and after a while to go into society, Margaret acting the part of a mother to her always.

CHAPTER IX.

" Why do I not marry?" answered Margaret reflectively. She was seated in Mrs. Hill's quiet little room. Five years had passed since her brother's death. Time had only increased her beauty, her sweet, serious eyes were sweeter and more serious than ever.

It was Sunday afternoon, she still spent those hours with her "friend." They were discoursing herself.

"You should marry, Margaret," Mrs. Hill had said; " you are lonely. Tell me why you have never married?"

"I don't think I can exactly tell you, dear friend," Margaret said after a pause. "I have never thought much of marriage in connection with myself. I have received offers of marriage, and I have several real friends among the men I know, but I have never cared more for one of them than another. And indeed I am not lonely. Since dear little Ida married I have been just a bit alone, but never lonely. Ida's husband is a lovely man, I think, and a very good one, too, if I am any judge of men. He will be good to her. Perhaps, if Val's baby had lived I might not have rejoiced so much in her marriage, but she was so young, and then my father never made her welcome. I don't think he wants any one but me."

"I have notions of my own about marriage," continued Margaret after a while. "If I had a husband he must do something besides love me. He must make me love him. He must command my respect and admiration, and must be real enough to keep them. He must teach me to understand and appreciate him. I don't believe in slavery of any kind, he must acknowledge me his equal. He must command my sympathy, I must feel about him in this way:

O noble soul, whose strength like mountains stand,
 Whose purposes, like adamantine stone
Bar roads to feeble feet, and wrap the land
 In sunny shadow, thou, too, hast thine own
 Sweet valleys full of flowers, for me alone,
Unseen, unknown, undreamed of by the mass
Who do not know the secret of the Pass.

"Shall I find this, do you think?" asked Margaret with a smile.

Her mother's eyes were full of tears.

"Men can be faithful; there is my father, for instance; my mother's memory is so precious, so sacred to him that he can never bear to speak of her. Something makes me stop when I begin to speak of her. I suppose her dear body rests in the family tomb, but there is no inscription, I suppose father could not bear even that. My father is a most peculiar man; even his love for me does not make me forget his want of love for poor Val. The one redeeming point in his whole nature to me is his reverence for my mother's memory."

Those hours spent with her child were life, heaven, to the silent, suffering mother. When Margaret first began to come, she said to herself: "She will soon tire of me; it will be natural. What have I to interest her?" So she calmed her delight; but she was mistaken, Margaret did not tire of her.

There was a fascination about this white-haired woman that she could not withstand; not that she tried to, it seemed natural to love her. Something in her sad eyes recalled that which she could not remember. Something there was in her kiss which seemed to beg for recollection.

"Dear Mrs. Hill," she said in the early days of their friendship, "perhaps it was in another world that I knew and loved you, you seem to have a right to my affection. My feelings for you are not like new feelings, rather like a continuation of something I have felt before. If my mother

3

was alive I might not care so much for you; it is hard to be motherless."

When Marie Stanhill was certain of her child's love, the temptation became stronger than ever to tell her the truth, but she did not yield to it. No, it was best as it was. What more did she want? Her child loved her as her most intimate friend, she confided her whole heart to her, and asked her advice in everything.

She even called her " little mother " in a tender, playful way. It would be easy to turn her heart from her father now—should she thus revenge herself upon the man who had been so hard and cruel to her? He had taken her child from her, and should she take her from him now? No! she would not do this. She must be entirely worthy of her daughter, nothing mean should dwell within her heart. She remembered a poem Margaret had read to her—Margaret was so fond of poetry—it was Helen Hunt Jackson's " Blind Spinner. " How her darling's voice had thrilled her as she read:

> " The bond divine I never doubt,
>   I know He set me here and still
>   And glad and blind I wait His will,
> But listen day by day
>   To hear their tread
> Who bear the finished web away
>   And cut the thread
> And bring God's message in the sun,
> Thou poor blind spinner, work is done. "

Marie Stanhill's nature had never become seared by her sorrows. Then her daily life among the sick and suffering was so full of les-

sons. Never did her sympathy fail those to
whom she ministered; sufferers read sincerity
in her gentle gaze. She did not weary of their
complaints; she tried always to comfort them,
each was to her a little child; her motherhood
folded around them like a mantle of protection.
She would bathe a burning head, or hold a
a fevered hand, and for that moment was the
mother.

One day Margaret went in search of her friend
at the hospital. She was directed to the woman's
ward. Stopping at the door she watched her for
a moment without making her presence known.

In her arms Marie held a new-born babe, she
was warming it against her breast, and she was
speaking to the young mother. Margaret drew
near that she might listen to what she was saying.
In after-years the sweet picture often came to her
and she would thank God for having been permitted to see it.

"You must not be blue, dearest," Marie's tender voice was saying. "You will soon be well,
God will give you back your strength, and you
must fight against evil for the little one's sake as
well as your own."

"What can I give it but a home among the
foundlings?" the young mother answered bitterly.
"It would be better off dead."

Then Marie spoke, and her whole soul came
into her face. Such tender words Margaret had
never dreamed of, she longed to kneel at the
white-haired woman's feet as she listened.

"God doesn't intend you to be wicked. This He gives you as a token of his love; this little white soul just from His soul. It is left to you; you may have its love. O, my child, do not desert it!"

As the young mother looked wistfully at her, the baby began to cry. She opened her arms and the nurse placed it upon her breast.

Turning away Marie saw her child.

"O, Mrs. Hill, I have heard your beautiful words, and I love you for them; love you more than ever, you sweet, tender mother. She," continued Margaret, "shall be added to my list."

Margaret Stanhill's list was a long one. Her wealth never went to public charities, she preferred a quiet mission. Through her friends she heard of many cases in which little interest was felt by the outside world.

"Are you troubled to-day that you came looking for me?" asked Marie with a loving smile, as she went with Margaret to a quiet part of the ward.

"Yes, I am going east to-morrow," said Margaret sadly. "My father insists that I must, and I don't want to go. I am growing to be an old woman, I dislike to have my life disturbed. If you were only going with me, then half of the battle would be over; I think it's leaving you that makes me hate to go so badly."

Then Marie began to cheer her, although her own heart was heavy at the thought of their separation.

CHAPTER X.

Three months later Margaret Stanhill again sat in her own room, after a return from the east, but no loneliness lies about her heart to-day. A wonderful thing has happened to her during these last three months. Love has crowned and perfected her womanhood. She had met William Kingsley at a reception a few days after her arrival in New York; there had immediately sprung up a feeling of interest and sympathy between them. They met almost every day, and the feeling of interest and sympathy grew into real friendship, and a warmer feeling soon followed. Margaret had gone to Long Branch. Kingsley remained in New York. A short separation revealed their real feelings for each other. When they met again each read love in the other's face and an engagement followed. There had been no hesitation about Margaret, she answered her lover's call gladly.

Mr. Stanhill could offer no objection to his daughter's choice; Mr. Kingsley was well born, well bred, and stood at the head of his profession. Margaret accepted her happiness thankfully. Only one thing seemed necessary to complete it, and that was to receive the congratulations of her dear friend, Mrs. Hill. There had been no time to write of the engagement; she was glad there had not been; the telling of it would be so much sweeter.

It was Sunday; she waited anxiously for the hour when she might go to her dear friend.

"You are pale," exclaimed Margaret, after their first embrace; "you have been ill and did not tell me of it."

"Nothing of any consequence," answered Marie quickly. "I shall be all right now that you are back again, how wonderfully well you look!" The mother-eye saw that something had come to her darling.

With a girlish blush Margaret told her secret, and then her happiness seemed complete.

Another week rolled by and Margaret was again seeking her friend's home on Mission street. She had been so happy all the week. To-morrow her "King" was to arrive! Her heart beat with anticipated joy; when next she took this trip he would walk beside her; she felt a strong desire for her lover and her friend to know each other.

CHAPTER XI.

Arriving at the house where her friend lived Margaret entered, and ran upstairs. She met no one; a stillness pervaded the house. Reaching the door of her friend's room she knocked; receiving no answer, she opened it and walked in. There sat her friend by the table; her white head bowed upon it. With a quick movement Margaret reached her side.

"Mrs. Hill! Little Mother! What is troubling you?" she cried.

'Great Heavens! She has fainted, thought Margaret, putting her hand upon her. She was very cold. She was dead. In her hand she clutched a pen; an ink-stand had been upset, and its contents had trickled on the table and dropped to the floor. Margaret lifted her head; it rested upon a little open book. She had been writing. Tenderly she drew the little book out and glanced at the last words. It seemed right for her to know what her dear friend's last thoughts had been. She read:

"O, my Margaret; mother's little Pearl! Mother is thankful for your happiness."

Mechanically she turned to the first page of the little book. It contained these words:

" Private Journal of Marie Stanhill. To be read by my children, Margaret and Valance, after my death. "

For a moment Margaret could not think: her brain seemed in a whirl. Was she mad? She read the words again. Then she could only think of one thing, that before her sat her mother whom she had believed to be dead all these years. Her revered mother. Silently she knelt at her feet, it seemed the only thing she could do. She asked for nothing else at that moment.

Then she remembered the last time she had seen her mother, and how clearly she heard her parting words.

"Mother! Mother!" she cried; then tears came to relieve her, and she sank sobbing upon the floor. To die thus unhappy and alone! O, had God no power that He refused to let her know in some way? She had been lost in her own love dream while her mother had been dropping her head upon the table in death. Now her place was here at her feet.

"O, darling, why did you not give me one little sign all these years?" she cried.

Then she remembered how she had been impelled to love her when as a nurse she stood beside Val's bed at the college, and how her presence had comforted her at his grave. O, how she blessed God for the instinct which had not let her throw away this precious mother.

Sweet, noble Margaret! No doubt arose in her heart of her mother's perfect worthiness; there was some terrible reason for her being here, for having left her children; for living under an assumed name, but she was not to blame for it. She thought of her father. Was he innocent also? If he had caused her mother to suffer she would punish him for it. She would avenge her mother.

She arose from her knees and taking the cold form in her strong young arms put it upon the bed; then kissing the icy lips she caressed her mother reverently. She must read this little book: every word of it. So she seated herselt beside the bed and opened it. It was told in a few words; this story of woman crucifixion. A man had suspected a woman of wrong doing; had accused her of dishonor; had deprived her of her children ; had driven her from home ; had not allowed her to defend herself.

That man was her father; that woman her mother! .She read the words: "I swear before God, my children, that I was innocent of even a wrong intention." Ah! her mother had no need to take such an oath. She would have believed her under any circumstances. One thought alone came to Margaret when she had learned all the book contained, she must take her mother back to the home from which she had been driven. A great strength came to her, she turned and looked at the clock, she had been here an hour. No one knew this, however; she must act as if she had just arrived. Putting the little book in her pocket, and the pen her mother had last touched also, she wiped as well as she could the ink from off the table. She wanted it to appear as if her mother had died in bed. Then she went into the hall and called for aid.

"My friend Mrs. Hill is unconscious; send quickly for a doctor; her doctor if you know him."

When the doctor arrived he said: "She is dead. I am not surprised; a few weeks ago I told her how it would be. It was heart trouble."

"Can you prevent an inquest? Can you give a certificate of . burial?" Then Margaret gave him her mother's real name. It was soon arranged, and an undertaker prepared everything.

In two hours Margaret followed the hearse bearing her mother's remains; it was taken to the

Stanhill residence. Margaret entered the house
and ordered the drawing-room to be opened. In
a few moments more Marie Stanhill lay in state
in the handsome apartment.

CHAPTER XII.

Valance Stanhill was hurrying home in answer
to a telephone from his daughter; as he reached
the gate he saw the crepe hanging upon it. In a
moment he stood beside Margaret.

"I have found my mother, and have brought
her home," was all she said.

Valance Stanhill staggered; then the old feeling of anger came back to him. "How dared
you?" he cried. "She is unfit."

But Margaret silenced him. "Stop, stop!"
she cried; "say one word against her, and I will
strike you! She is my mother, and one of God's
holiest martyrs."

She put her hand in her pocket and drew from
it the little book.

"Read this! You do not deserve it. I only
give it to you that your punishment may begin."

He took it and turned to leave the room.

"Understand, once for all, that I believe every
word of it," she cried.

*   *   *   *   *   *   *

The hour for the funeral was approaching;
crowds of people were flocking to the house. A
notice of the death of Marie, wife of Valance
Stanhill, was inserted in the paper at Margaret's

command. Such a mystery! How society did
wonder and talk.

Margaret sat by her mother's coffin, draped in
deepest mourning; .beside her stood her be-
trothed; he had arrived the day before. Margaret had explained things briefly to him.

"If you dislike what I have done," she said
proudly, "you can leave immediately." His
only answer had been to take her in his arms.
Together they had gone to the silent mother.

"Mother," said Margaret pitifully, "this is my
husband. O, mother, I am not mistaken in him !
Look down from heaven and bless him." Then
he, whom she loved, bent and kissed the dead
woman's lips.

Valance Stanhill had not been seen; he was in
his room. People continued to whisper and wonder. The minister arrived, he assumed his
flowing vestment, and entered the room, the
ceremony was about to begin. At that moment
the bowed figure of the master of the house entered the room and came and stood beside the
coffin. He looked at the white face with its
crown of snowy hair, then knelt beside it. He
paid no attention to the curious people.

"Marie," he whispered, "Marie, my wife,
forgive me! O, forgive me!" He bowed his
head and began to sob.

Margaret went to him. "Father," she whispered, "you are forgiven, look at her face."

He looked and was comforted.

All the sadness and pain seemed to have left

the dead woman's face, and a sweet, peaceful smile had spread itself over her features. And the people looked and wondered.

The old family vault was opened and Marie Stanhill's coffin was placed beside that of her son's.

As the last bit of plaster was put on the opening, Valance Stanhill stepped forward and picked up a piece of stone, and with it wrote on the soft surface:

"Marie, beloved, honored wife of Valance Stanhill."

Thus was the last thread cut in the web of Marie Stanhill's life, and she received

> "God's message in the sun,
> Thou poor blind spinner, work is done."